Finding Me
By Derrica Wilson

Illustrated by Fatma Topal

Copyright © 2022 by Derrica Wilson
All rights reserved. This book or any portion there of may not be reproduced or used in any manner whatsoever without the express written permission of the Author except for the use of brief quotations in a book review.

Have You Seen Me?

I looked down at the poster in my hands, lifting one up to pin it to the telephone pole. Coby yapped at my side, climbing on his hind legs while I hung the poster.

"We'll find her," I said, patting his head, "We'll bring her home."

"Officer Carlise!" someone shouted. A young girl jogged toward me, the wind kicking up the beads on the ends of her braids. A stack of posters were clutched between her fingers. She stopped and held them out to me. "You left these in the printer."

"Thank you, Daisa," I said. I handed her Coby's leash, and we continued down the sidewalk together, pinning the posters to every pole and community announcement board we saw.

No one has seen Sierra Knight in fifteen days. The Bay has been in a frenzy since her parents reported her missing.

"Do you think we'll find her, Officer Carlise?" Daisa asked, taping a poster to a coffee shop window.

"I hope so," I replied, "We've got some detectives coming in to help with the investigation. We will start briefing tomorrow."
Daisa lifted an eyebrow, "What's briefing?"

"It's when I, along with the rest of Willow Bay's police department will go over the details of the case with new detectives. We'll give them all of the evidence we have so we can begin to work this case together."

We continued down main street, handing posters to a few of the people we passed. An hour later, our hands were empty. I drove Daisa home and made my way to mine.

I thought about Sierra while I made dinner, wondering where she might be, and I was determined to find her. Whatever it took, I was ready.

Name: Sierra Knight
Age: 12
Height: 5'2
Weight: 140lbs
Last Seen: 12/20/2021
Last Seen Wearing: Beige Sweater, Dark Jeans, and White Converse

I went over the description as Sierra photo glowed on the TV screen in the conference room. Honey brown eyes resting beautifully against her dark skin. She was smiling in the photo her mother chose.

Our neighboring jurisdiction sent three officers: Detective Alstead, Detective Reams, and Detective Frasier.

"Here's what we know so far," I said, "Sierra was last seen outside Willow Bay high school. The buildings outside cameras caught her walking along the far side of the building. She rounds this corner here," I pointed at the screen, "And vanishes."

"Is there another camera that catches someone grabbing her or her getting into a vehicle?" Detective Reams asked.

"No," I replied, "Unfortunately the cameras on this side of the building were broken by the recent storms. They haven't gotten around to repairing them."
Detective Alstead scribbled a few notes on his memo pad, "First order of business then."
I nodded, "Absolutely."

"I think it's time for a press conference. We can address the city as a whole and ask for help in solving the case." Detective Frasier said.

"A good idea, Frasier," Reams replied, "But do you think the community will be willing to help us?"

The room was silent for a moment and each of us pondered this question. Relations between Willow Bay and its law enforcement haven't been the greatest. Our community is made up of mostly black and brown people. Racial tensions have been high, trust has been low, and it's been difficult to mend the burned bridges.

"A young girl is missing," I said, "I think rallying together to find her will bolster some support in the community. We need to show them that this department is not to be feared, that we're truly here to protect and serve."

Daisa was waiting outside the conference room after the briefing.

"Don't you have school?" I said with a smile.

She took a few folders out of my arms and helped me carry them back to my office, "I had study hall last period. My mom dropped me off here. How was the briefing?"

"It went well, we're going to get the cameras at the back of your school replaced, and we're going to do a press conference today."

"Will that help?" Daisa asked.

"It could. It'll show Willow Bay that we're here to help."

When we got to my office, Daisa set the folders down on the desk. She sat down in the chair across from me, tucking her legs beneath her, "Officer Carlise."
"Yes?"

"Some kids were talking at lunch…" she began, "Sierra's friend Alana said that Sierra had a boyfriend. An older boyfriend."
"And where did she meet this boyfriend?"

"On this website called WeSpeak. You log on and video chat with strangers."
"You know that's incredibly dangerous, right Daisa?"
"Yes. I'm not on it, my parents have it blocked, but tons of kids at school use it all of the time."

Daisa continued to explain how Sierra said that her and the boyfriend are in love, and they were going to run away together.

After Daisa's mom picked her up, I called the detectives into my office.

"We may have a lead," I said.

Detective Alstead contacted Sierra's parents and called them down to the station. They brought Sierra's laptop and we were able to gain access to her We Speak account. She had one frequent "speaker", an account with the name *Romeo818*.

After Sierra's parents went home, Detective Reams reached out to We Speak's tech department and requested the contact information on the account.

"They'll get back to us within 24-hours," he said.

I nodded, "Good, let's regroup after the press conference tomorrow."

"Our phone lines are open 24/7!" I said into the microphone, "Anyone with information to help us find Sierra Knight, please don't hesitate to call."

Reporters swarmed the stage, and the three detectives volunteered to answer their questions while I went to the group of students gathered by the information booth.

"Officer Carlise," one student said, "You mentioned that kids being on We Speak is dangerous, why do you think that is?"

"Because of situations like this," I said softly, "There are people online that take advantage of young people, lying to them and convincing them to participate in harmful activities."

"What if we just don't meet them in person?" another student said.

"That's always the option, but even talking to these people online is dangerous. They can trick you into giving them your personal information."

"It's best if we avoid talking to strangers online," Daisa said, "Even if their intentions could be good in the long run, most times it's incredibly dangerous."

I slipped out of the crowd when my radio went off, leaving Daisa to address her classmates' questions. I smiled at her. She was certainly holding her own.
"We've got him," Detective Frasier scratched over the radio. My head flew up and I searched the crowd, finding the detectives grouped together at the edge of the lot. I jogged over to them, "You found him?"

"We Speak got back to us. The users legal name is Roland Isaac. He did six years upstate for assault," Reams said.

"His last known address is about half an hour from here," Alstead added.

"Let's go," I said.

We climbed into our cars, turned on our sirens, and headed out. We arrived at an abandoned house. Some of the windows were shattered, and the door was swinging open.

Other officers arrived on the scene and surrounded the house.
We moved in slowly, apprehending the suspect as he was trying to escape from the first-floor window.

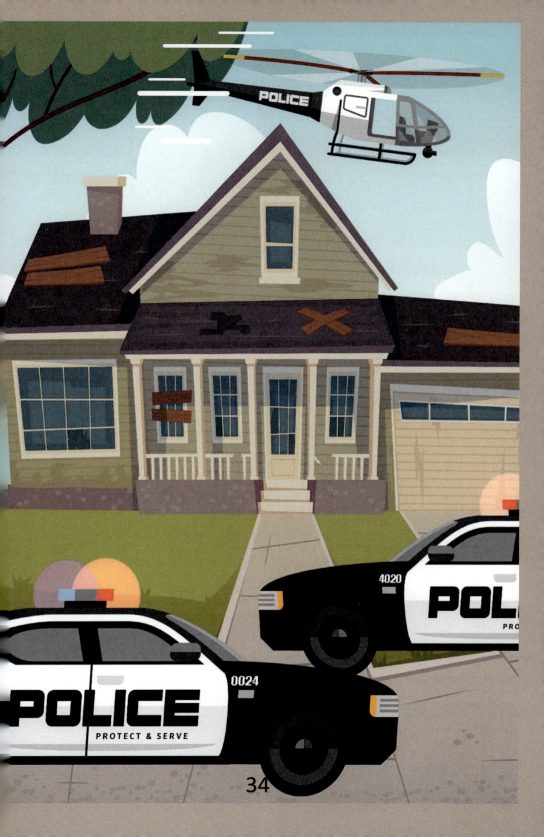

In a bedroom at the back of a hallway, Sierra was in a fetal position on the floor. Her clothes were torn, and her face was dirty. A single cut on top of her forehead.

"It's okay, you're safe," I said, walking toward her slowly.
We took Sierra to the hospital and called her parents. Thankfully, she was relatively unharmed.

Detective Alstead and I sat down with Sierra and her parents in her hospital room.

"Can you tell us what happened, Sierra?" Detective Alstead said.

"I've been talking to Ronald on WeSpeak for a month now. I'd log on and we'd video chat for a few hours every night. He told me he loved me, and that we could get married and live together. When I finished school that day, he told me to meet him at the back of the school."

"And you got in the car with him?" I said gently.

Sierra nodded, "He smiled at me at first, but the next thing I know, I'm being blindfolded by someone in the backseat. They took me to that house and locked me in the bedroom."

As Sierra continued to tell her story, we learned that the men were planning to sell her. That their job was getting young girls and selling them to other men.

The doctor came in and cleared Sierra to go home, but she protested.

"Officer Carlise, I'd like to go and see my friends."

I drove Sierra to the park where we hosted the press conference. Their signs sporting

Welcome Home, Sierra and *We Missed You.*

Some families brought food and drinks, and soon, the press conference transitioned into a block party. Students and friends dancing in the streets. Sierra in the middle of it all, laughing and smiling like she was meant to.

We found her, and we brought her home.

Made in the USA
Monee, IL
11 March 2022